This book belongs to

....

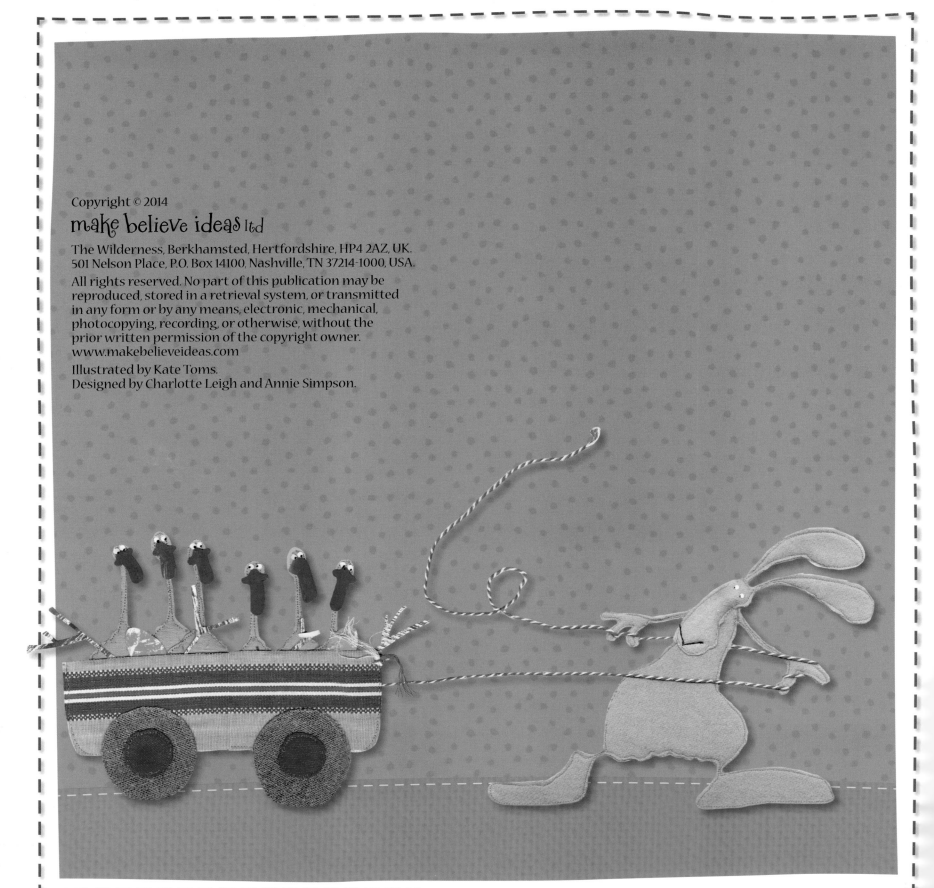

The Twelve Days of Christmas

Kate Toms

1 2 3 4 5 6

7 8 9 10 11 12

make
believe
ideas

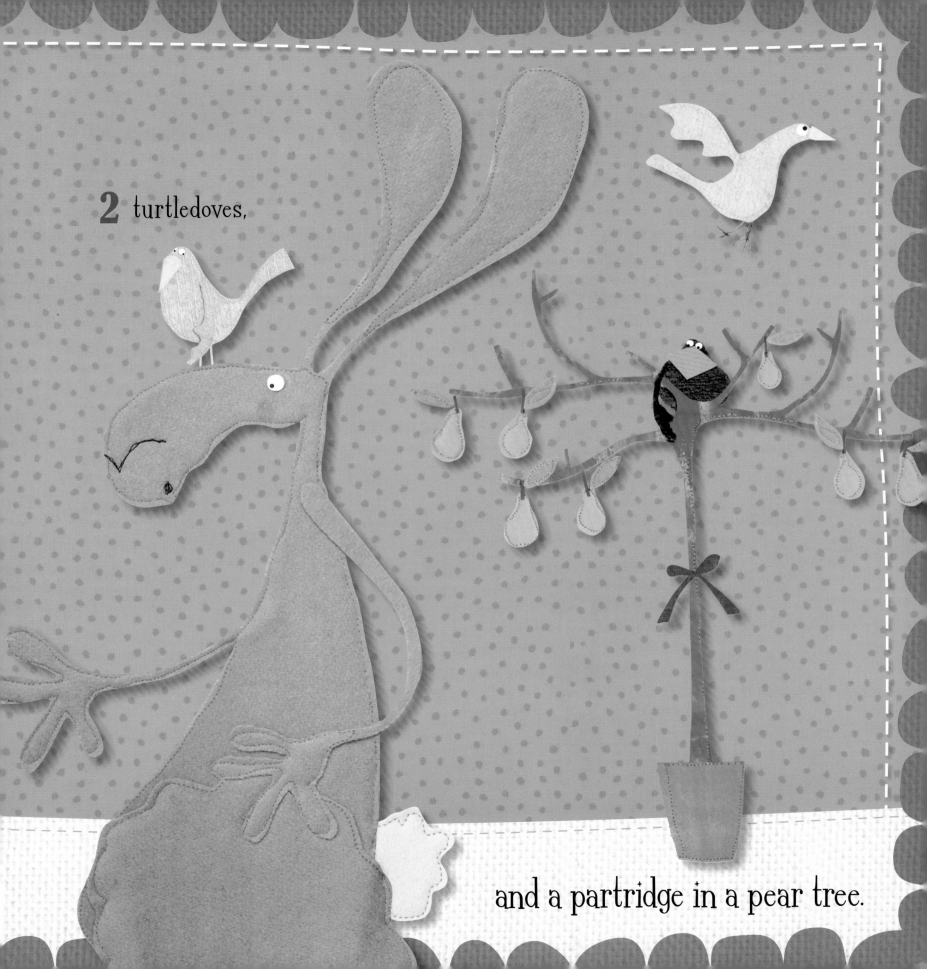

2 turtledoves,

and a partridge in a pear tree.

On the 4th day of Christmas, my true love sent to me . . .

4 calling birds,

2 turtledoves,

3 French hens,

and a partridge in a pear tree.

On the 5th day of Christmas,
my true love
sent to me . . .

5 gold rings,

Gold Rings

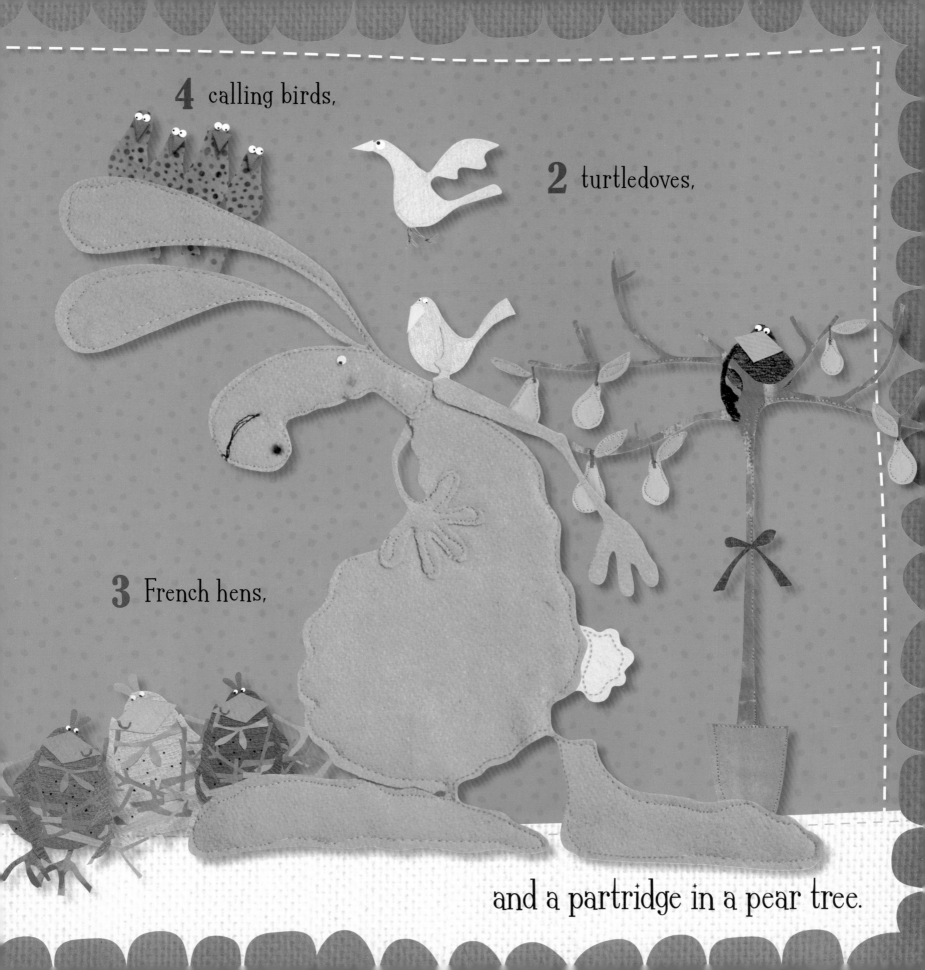

4 calling birds,

2 turtledoves,

3 French hens,

and a partridge in a pear tree.

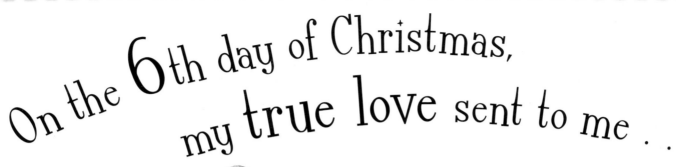

On the 6th day of Christmas,
my true love sent to me . . .

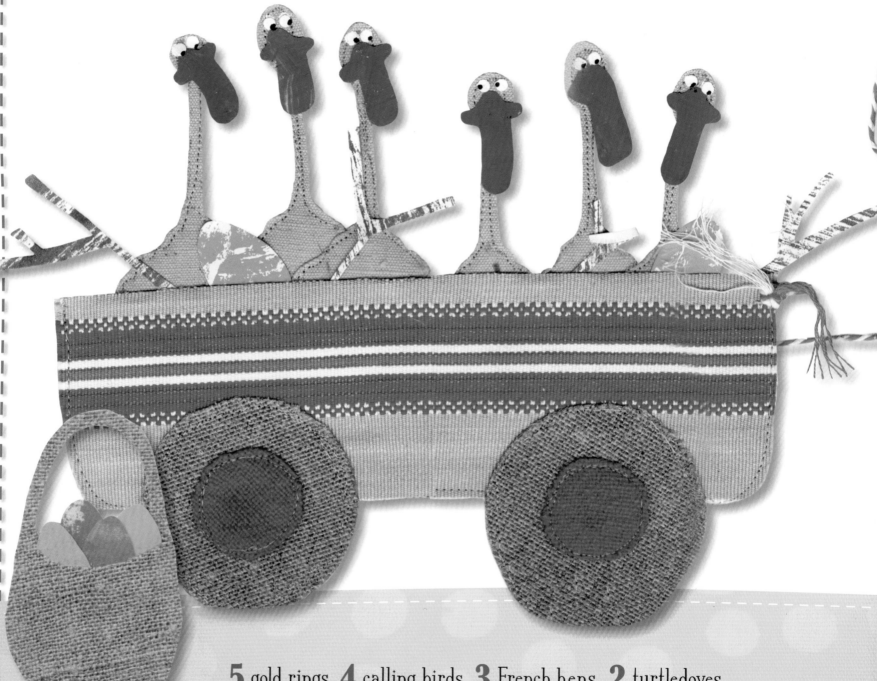

5 gold rings, **4** calling birds, **3** French hens, **2** turtledoves,

6 geese-a-laying,

and a partridge in a pear tree.

squawk!

On the 7th day of Christmas, my true love sent to me . . . .

7 swans-a-swimming,

6 geese-a-laying, **5** gold rings, **4** calling birds, **3** French hens, **2** turtledoves,

and a partridge in a pear tree.

squawk!

On the **8**th day of Christmas,
my **true** love sent to me . . .

7 swans-a-swimming, **6** geese-a-laying, **5** gold rings,
4 calling birds, **3** French hens, **2** turtledoves,

8 maids-a-milking,

and a partridge in a pear tree.

squawk!

On the **9**th day of Christmas,
my true love sent to me . . . .

8 maids-a-milking, **7** swans-a-swimming, **6** geese-a-laying,
5 gold rings, **4** calling birds, **3** French hens, **2** turtledoves,

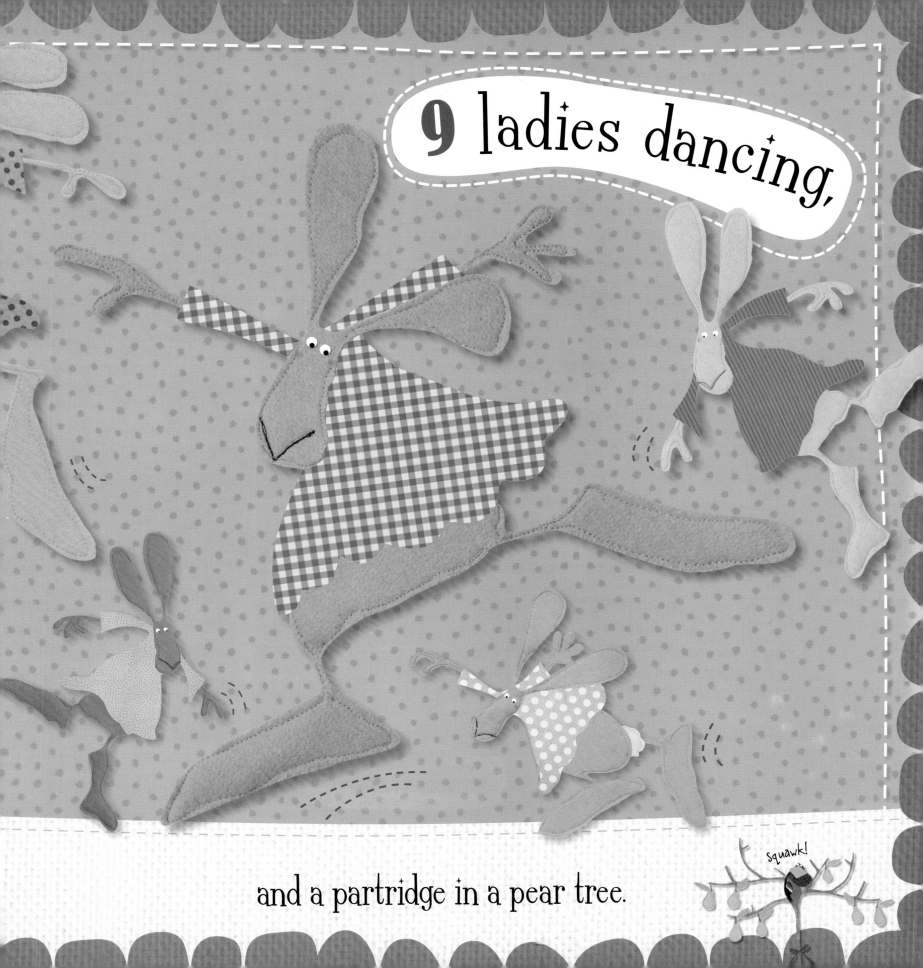

9 ladies dancing,

and a partridge in a pear tree.

squawk!

On the 10th day of Christmas, my true love sent to me . . .

9 ladies dancing, 8 maids-a-milking, 7 swans-a-swimming, 6 geese-a-laying, 5 gold rings, 4 calling birds, 3 French hens, 2 turtledoves,

10 lords-a-leaping,

and a partridge in a pear tree.

squawk!

On the **11**th day of Christmas,
my true love
sent to me . . .

10 lords-a-leaping, **9** ladies dancing, **8** maids-a-milking, **7** swans-a-swimming,
6 geese-a-laying, **5** gold rings, **4** calling birds, **3** French hens, **2** turtledoves,

On the 12th day of Christmas,
my true love sent to me . . . .

12 drummers drumming,

11 pipers piping, 10 lords-a-leaping, 9 ladies dancing, 8 maids-a-milking, 7 swans-a-swimming,

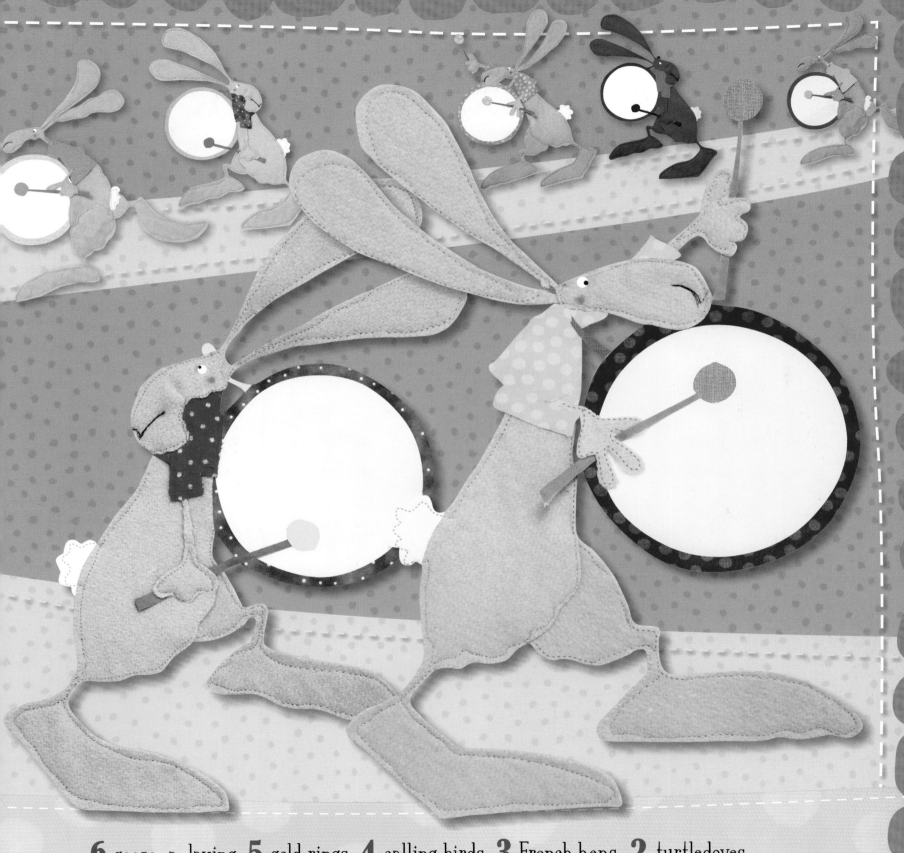

6 geese-a-laying, 5 gold rings, 4 calling birds, 3 French hens, 2 turtledoves, . . .

. . . and a partridge in a pear tree.